For Rebecca Spens

A Red Fox Book

Published by Random House Children's Books
20 Vauxhall Bridge Road, London SW1V 2SA

A division of The Random House Group Ltd
London Melbourne Sydney Auckland
Johannesburg and agencies throughout the world

1 3 5 7 9 10 8 6 4 2

First published in Great Britain in 1997 by
The Bodley Head Children's Books
Red Fox edition 2001

Printed in Hong Kong by Midas Printing Ltd

THE RANDOM HOUSE GROUP Limited Reg. No. 954009

www.randomhouse.co.uk

ISBN 0-09-969261-9

Ellie's Breakfast

Ellie's Breakfast

Sarah Garland

RED FOX

Dad!

Come on, Ellie.

It's time for breakfast.

Breakfast for the rabbits.

Breakfast for the turkeys.

Breakfast for the ducks.

Breakfast for the goats.

The goats don't want their breakfast.

The goats want Ellie's hat!

Look out, Ellie!

But Ellie needs the hat

to carry the eggs...

for Dad to cook...

for Ellie's breakfast.